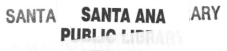

D0389890

## Other titles in the bunch:

Big Dog and Little Dog Go Sailing

Big Dog and Little Dog Visit the Moon

Colin and the Curly Claw

Dexter's Journey

Follow the Swallow

"Here I Am!" said Smedley

Horrible Haircut

Magic Lemonade

The Magnificent Mummies

Midnight in Memphis

Peg

Shoot!

## Crabtree Publishing Company
**www.crabtreebooks.com**

PMB 16A, 350 Fifth Avenue
Suite 3308
New York, NY 10118

612 Welland Avenue
St. Catharines, Ontario
Canada, L2M 5V6

Fearnley, Jan.
  Colin and the Curly Claw / Jan Fearnley.
    p. cm. -- (Blue Bananas)
  Summary: When Colin and his mother visit the dinosaur exhibit at
the museum, Colin ends up going home with a dinosaur's claw, and
its owner wants it back.
    ISBN 0-7787-0840-3 -- ISBN 0-7787-0886-1 (pbk.)
  [1. Dinosaurs--Fiction. 2. Museums--Fiction. 3. Mothers and
sons--Fiction. 4. London (England)--Fiction. 5. England--Fiction. 6.
Humorous stories.] I. Title. II. Series
PZ7.F2965 Co 2002
[E]--dc21

2001032435
LC

Published by Crabtree Publishing in 2002
First published in 2001 by Mammoth
an imprint of Egmont Children's Books Limited
Text and Illustrations copyright © Jan Fearnley 2001
The Author and Illustrator have asserted their moral rights.
Paperback ISBN 0-7787-0886-1
Reinforced Hardcover Binding ISBN 0-7787-0840-3

# COLIN
## and the
## CURLY CLAW

### Jan Fearnley

## Blue Bananas

For Izaak and Emily

J.F.

At 34 Anderson Street, Colin woke up feeling

very excited.

Today he was going on a trip to the museum.

Colin loved museums.

Colin washed his face, even behind his ears.

He brushed his teeth, without being told twice!

Then he quickly got dressed.

He ate all his porridge – even the lumpy
bits – yuk!

Then he waited ages for his mom to get
ready. She was doing all that mom stuff.

At last, they set off.

The bus chugged and rumbled its way through the town until they came to the very last stop.

The museum stop.

Mom gave Colin the money for his ticket.

He dashed up the steps. He couldn't wait to

get inside!

"Remember to say thank you," his mom called.

The turnstile creaked as Colin pushed it

with all his might.

They went down the long, polished,

echoing corridor.

It was dark and smelled of beeswax and old

ladies' purses.

"Don't run off," said his mom, clomping

along behind.

11

They looked at the paintings.

They looked at the shiny suits of armor.

They looked at the Egyptian mummies.

They looked at the sculptures.

They looked at the big woolly mammoth.

It raised its trunk in salute and seemed to

point the way towards a sign . . .

TO THE DINOSAURS.

Colin sucked in his cheeks with anticipation.

His mouth made a big "OOOH!" shape.

*This* was what he wanted to see more than

anything else.

15

He clattered down the dark and dusty corridor.

The dinosaurs were waiting for him.

"Not too fast!" said his mom.

Then she spotted Mrs. Bakewell from down the

street and stopped to chat.

Colin was all alone . . .

. . . except, of course, for the dinosaurs.

Colin looked at the dinosaur skeletons.

Big skeletons and little skeletons and teeny, tiny skeletons.

Fat skeletons and thin skeletons and shiny, flat fossils.

Every kind of dinosaur was there.

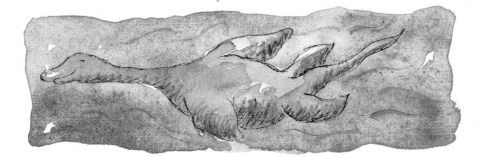

Flying ones, swimming ones, even ones that

moved, like they do on television.

And there, in the corner all on its own, stood . . .

. . . the best dinosaur of all.

A powerful spotlight, as strong as the moon, lit

its yellow bumpy skin.

One big foot rested on a log, as the dinosaur

stood proudly.

Its big, bony head was held high in

the air. Its tiny eyes twinkled.

It had hundreds of dagger teeth that smiled a clever smile and on each hand there was a huge, curly claw.

It was magnificent. It was beautiful. It was so cool!

You'd better believe it, baby!

A sign said: "Do not touch the exhibit", but Colin couldn't resist a closer look.

The dinosaur's bright eyes sparkled, the fearsome claws gleamed in the light.

Colin reached out his hand . . . and stroked one of the claws very gently with the tip of his finger.

And it FELL OFF!

OH NO! What have I done?

It dropped, like a big, ripe nut, right into the palm of his hand! Colin looked around. His cheeks were burning. His fingers curled around the claw. He quickly put it in his pocket and went to find his mom.

Now all he wanted was to get out of there.

Colin tried not to think about the claw but it was always there, lurking in his head.

He tried to concentrate really hard on his swimming lesson.

He worked so hard that his mom took
him to the fair as a treat. This was
fantastic. Colin began to feel a lot better.

There was just time to do some shopping

for supper before they caught the bus home.

29

By evening, Colin had almost forgotten
about the claw.

But, as he swung, back and forth, back and
forth, Colin was sure he could hear a
strange voice calling him.

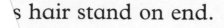

s hair stand on end.

Who took my curly claw?
Who took my curly claw?
Someone took my curly claw!
I THINK IT'S YOU!

Colin looked around. There was nobody to be seen.

I must have imagined it.

The voice growled again . . .

who took my curly claw?

Who took my curly claw?

someone took my curly claw!

I THINK IT'S YOU!

Colin ran up the garden path and

hammered on the door.

He could still hear the voice . . . it was

following him!

Oh, no!

Who took my curly claw?
Who took my curly claw?
Someone took my curly claw!
I THINK IT'S YOU!

His mom opened the door. Colin dashed in.

"Hey! Where's the fire?" Mom said.

My, you're eager to go to bed!

He's coming!

Colin sprinted up the stairs, fast as a rabbit.

Thud, thud, thud, went his feet.

Boom diddy boom went his heart.

And all the time, that voice was

getting closer . . .

Who took my curly claw?
Who took my curly claw?
Someone took my curly claw!
I THINK IT'S YOU!

Colin reached his room and dived under
the covers.

All the time, the voice was calling . . .

Colin tucked the covers right over his head.
Now there were footsteps on the stairs, the
slow, careful tread of something big coming
to gobble him up!

The door opened . . . CREEEAAAK!

It was his mom!

"I thought you were a dinosaur!" Colin cried.

In bed, Colin reached under the quilt and gave his mom the curly claw.

"It's a real dinosaur claw," he said in a small voice.

"Very nice dear," said his mom, putting

the claw in her pocket.

"We'll take it back tomorrow."

Colin sighed and settled down. His

mom read a story.

"Goodnight," she said when they got to

the end.

After a long bath, Mom popped the claw

into the pocket of her favorite bathrobe and

went downstairs.

"Dinosaurs indeed!" She chuckled to herself.

"That boy has such an imagination."

42

She made herself a mug of hot chocolate.

She got herself a cookie.

And settled down for the night.

The next day, the curator of the museum was very angry.

"What has happened to my best exhibit?" he said.

He took my bathrobe!

Where **did** those clothes come from?

The dinosaur didn't move but he seemed to
be standing even prouder than usual, from
the top of his noble head right down to the
tips of his nicely painted claws.

The dinosaur was more popular than ever!

Only Colin and his mom knew exactly

what had happened.

But *they* weren't going to tell, not ever.